D1207909

World of Fairy Tales

Hansel and Gretel
and
The Pied Piper of Hamelin

Two Tales and Their Histories

alphabet
soup

an imprint of

WINDMILL
BOOKS

New York

Published in 2010 by Windmill Books, LLC
303 Park Avenue South, Suite # 1280, New York, NY 10010-3657

Adaptations to North American Edition © 2010 Windmill Books

Editor (Arcturus): Carron Brown
Designer: Steve Flight

Library of Congress Cataloging-in-Publication Data

Brown, Carron.
    Hansel and Gretel and The Pied Piper of Hamelin: two tales and their histories / Carron Brown.—
1st North American ed.
        p. cm.— (World of fairy tales)
Summary: A retelling, accompanied by a brief history, of the two well-known tales in the first of
which a lost brother and sister meet a wicked witch in the forest and, in the second, the Pied Piper
exacts a terrible revenge on the greedy citizens of Hamelin.
    ISBN 978-1-60754-646-7 (library binding)—ISBN 978-1-60754-647-4 (pbk.)
    ISBN 978-1-60754-648-1 (6-pack)
    1. Fairy tales. [1. Fairy tales. 2. Pied Piper of Hamelin (Legendary character)—Legends. 3.
Folklore—Germany.] I. Pied Piper of Hamelin. English. II. Title. III. Title: Hansel and Gretel and The
Pied Piper of Hamelin. IV. Title: Pied Piper of Hamelin.
    PZ8.B697Han 2010
    [398.2]—dc22

                                    2009037519

Printed in China

CPSIA Compliance Information: Batch #AW0102W: For further information contact Windmill Books, New York, New York at 1-866-478-0556.

For more great fiction and nonfiction, go to windmillbooks.com.

Hansel and Gretel

ONCE UPON A TIME, LONG AGO, A POOR WOODCUTTER lived with his family in a little house made of wood and thatch, at the edge of a great enchanted forest. His first wife had died and he had remarried a woman who was always in a bad mood. Nevertheless, he was happy he had two lovely children from his first marriage: a good and brave son called Hansel and a beautiful daughter called Gretel.

One year, the country was
hit by a terrible famine.
When winter came, the poor
woodcutter had no food.

"What is going to happen to us?
We have no bread. We must find food quickly,
or we will die of hunger," said the woodcutter, sadly.
Then, his cruel wife had a terrible idea:
"Tomorrow we will take Hansel and Gretel deep into the
enchanted forest and leave them there. They will never
find their way home and we shall be well rid of
them! Then we will have two mouths less to
feed..."

4

"But I couldn't do such a thing! They are my children," cried the woodcutter.

"So you'd prefer to die!" his wife replied harshly.

The poor woodcutter cried a thousand tears but, terrified of his wicked wife's temper, he gave in. In the next room, Hansel and Gretel, who were supposed to be asleep, heard their stepmother's cruel words. Little Gretel began to sob:

"Oh, my brother, I don't want to be left in that terrible forest. I am so frightened of witches!"

Hansel took his little sister in his arms, hugged her tight and comforted her.

"Don't be afraid, little sister. Grandfather taught me how to track our way home. We'll get out of it!"

During the night, Hansel got out of bed. Making sure that his father and stepmother were fast asleep, he crept into the garden, gathered some small white pebbles, then went back to bed without making a sound. Early next morning, their stepmother opened the children's bedroom door and called:

"Come on, up you get, you lazybones! We are going to gather wood in the forest!"

Gretel blinked back her tears. In his pocket Hansel held tight to the little pebbles. The cruel stepmother ran through the enchanted forest. Hansel followed her, throwing down his precious white pebbles behind him as he went. After a very long walk, the wicked stepmother stopped.

"Stay beneath that tree and when I have finished working I will come back for you," she said in a soft, dishonest voice.

Hansel knew that their horrible
stepmother was lying, and that she would not
return. He lay down under the tree with his
little sister. Shivering with cold, they fell asleep.
When Hansel and Gretel awoke, it was night
and no one had come to fetch them. An
icy wind was blowing and Gretel began
to cry because she was so frightened.

"Be brave, Gretel," said Hansel. "When
the moon shines we will be able to see the pebbles
that I threw on the path. We will find our way back and be home
by morning." The two children walked all night through the forest,
following the trail of pebbles, hoping that they would not meet any
witches. They arrived home at dawn. The woodcutter was wild
with joy to see them. Hansel and Gretel were
so happy to be back with their father
that they forgot all about
being tired and hungry.

But when she saw them, their stepmother was angry:

"Where have you been, you brats? You disobeyed me! Your father and I have been sick with worry!"

Hansel and Gretel did not answer their stepmother, which only increased her rage. Exhausted, they went to their bedroom to rest. The stepmother waited a few moments, pushed open the bedroom door to make sure the children were asleep, then she spoke to her husband:

"Tomorrow morning we will take them even further into the enchanted forest and this time Hansel and Gretel will be lost forever. They will never find their way home and we shall be well rid of them!"

The unhappy woodcutter tried to protest, but his wife started shouting:

"Look around you! We have nothing to eat. All that's left is one tiny crust of bread. I am not going to die of hunger because of your greedy children."

The woodcutter shed a thousand tears, but he gave in to his wife once more. Fortunately, Hansel had overheard their conversation. He tried to go out into the garden to look for pebbles again, but this time, the house door was locked. So he went back to bed to think of another idea. Next day, before the sun rose, the stepmother went to wake the children. She gave each of them a tiny piece of bread and then led them even deeper than before into the enchanted forest.

Since Hansel had no pebbles this time, he threw crumbs from his piece of bread onto the path.

When night fell, Hansel and Gretel were alone once more, abandoned in the heart of the forest. The moon began to shine and the two children looked everywhere for the breadcrumbs which were meant to show them the way home. Alas, the birds had eaten all the crumbs! There was no trace of them! The children wandered for three long days and three long nights, completely lost in the huge forest. Exhausted and starving, Gretel fell to the ground.

"We are lost and we are going to be eaten by witches," she said, crying. Despite being brave, Hansel was also frightened. Horrible things were said about the forest witches. Not knowing what to do, he and Gretel lay down to rest. Next morning, the tuneful song of a robin awoke the children. Hansel took his little sister by the hand and they set out to find their way home. They hadn't gone far before they saw smoke coming out of a chimney. There was a house nearby and someone was at home.

"We are saved! We are saved!" cried the children.

As they approached the house, they saw to their
delight that it was made entirely of candy and cake.
The roof was tiled in chocolate. The chimney was
made of nougat. And the walls were gingerbread, coated with jelly.

Hansel loved nougat, so he climbed onto the roof
and ate up part of the chimney. Gretel greedily
licked the walls covered with
jelly. They had never eaten such
delicious things! But suddenly
they heard a strange voice
from inside the house:

"Nibble-mouse, nibble-mouse, who is nibbling at my house?"

"It's the wind! It's the wind!" the children replied, laughing.

"It sounds more like children to me. And I love children. So come in and sit down at my table and I'll serve you a feast fit for a king!"

Hansel and Gretel were still hungry, so they rushed into the kitchen. The door banged shut and a horrible witch stood before them. Her back was hunched, her teeth were black, her hair was like spiders' webs, and there was a large wart on her ugly nose. The witch caught Hansel by the arm and threw him into a cage. Then she tied Gretel to the table leg.

"Hee! Hee! Hee!" she cackled. "Now it's my turn for a feast. I'm going to eat you but, so that I enjoy you even better, I'll wait until I have fattened you up."

For the first few days, Hansel and Gretel managed not to eat the witch's sweets. But after a while, Hansel was so hungry that he gobbled everything she gave him.

After a week, Hansel had become quite plump and the horrible witch decided he was now fat enough to become her dinner.

"Oh! Wonderful! This boy promises to be … tasty!" she hissed greedily.

She lit the fire to cook poor Hansel. He was trembling with fear. Then she untied Gretel, who seemed just as scared as Hansel.

"Climb into that oven, girl," she said,
"and tell me if it is hot enough to cook your brother in. Hee! Hee! Hee!"

"But I have never been in an oven before. Can you help me?" asked Gretel.

"Stupid girl! The oven door is so big that I could get in myself."

So saying, the cruel witch climbed into the oven. Gretel quickly slammed the oven door tight. The witch began to burn, and screamed horribly. Gretel grabbed the cage key and set Hansel free.

"I've thrown the witch into the oven, she is dead, we are free!" she cried, hugging her brother.

In the witch's living room stood a shining chest. Curious, Hansel and Gretel opened it. Inside they found magnificent jewels and sacks filled with countless gold pieces. They'd never seen so much treasure in a single place!

The children filled their pockets with the treasure and ran off. In the forest, the sun was shining. Hansel and Gretel finally found their way home. When they arrived, their father could not hold back his tears, he was so happy. He had felt lonely without his children, and their wicked stepmother was dead!

Gretel untied her dress and thousands of diamonds fell out. Hansel turned out his pockets and a shower of gold pieces tumbled onto the floor. Thus, with all the witch's money, they never knew hunger or were poor again, and for many years afterwards, Hansel and Gretel lived happily with their father on the edge of the enchanted forest.

THE END

The Pied Piper
of Hamelin

ONCE UPON A TIME, A LONG TIME AGO, THERE WAS
a small town in Germany called Hamelin. It was a fine town
of rich merchants and wealthy traders. The people wanted for
nothing: their granaries were full of corn and their cellars had the
biggest barrels of wine in the region. Life in Hamelin was good.

Then, one day, a terrible disaster struck the town. A big, black rat appeared. It had a pointed nose and red eyes. At first, the townsfolk did not pay it much attention. But then a second rat arrived, then a third, then a fourth! Within a few days, the town was overrun by thousands of rats. The streets, squares, even the houses were swarming with the nasty creatures. These rats were not afraid of anything.

They fought the dogs, bit the horses, attacked the cats, and when people tried to chase them away with a broom or a shovel, they came back moments later in even greater numbers.

18

The situation was dreadful. The townsfolk became more and more worried, so they called a meeting in the town hall square, to find a solution.

"This can't go on," one of them said. "The rats are eating up everything. Soon we won't have any food left in our winter stores!"

"Before the rats came, Hamelin was a clean, quiet town. Look at the mess these creatures have made," added another.

"We must drive out the rats as quickly as possible. This has gone on too long," they all shouted together.

The crowd was becoming restless. In order to calm them down, the mayor of Hamelin came out of the town hall and addressed them:

"Dear fellow townsfolk, we are going through a difficult time. But I am sure that in the end these rats will leave the town."

"Well, just what are you going to do to get rid of them?" demanded the unhappy people.

"I'm going to call together my councillors to come to a decision," he replied.

But the townsfolk of Hamelin had already waited too long and demanded an end to the problem. Saying the first thing that came into his head, the mayor took out a big purse from his pocket and said:

"Here is a purseful of gold. I am prepared to give it to the person who will get rid of the rats for us."

A great silence fell on the square. People were busy thinking about what they could do with a purseful of gold. But none of the townsfolk of Hamelin actually knew how to get rid of the rats. Just then, a voice spoke from the middle of the crowd.

"I—the Pied Piper—am prepared to take on the challenge."

Everybody looked with surprise at the one who had just spoken. It was the first time he had been seen in the town. Tall and slender, the man had strange piercing eyes and a long, very thin moustache. He wore strange clothes, too, in bright colors, and held a flute between his fingers.

"Can you get rid of all the rats in the town for us?" asked the mayor, amazed.

"Certainly. And they won't ever come back," said the stranger.

The townsfolk of Hamelin were speechless. The mayor himself did
not know what to think.

"Well, since you know what to do, get to work! What are you
waiting for?" he said.

"First we must settle one last detail. That purseful of gold seems but
poor payment to me. I demand a gold piece for each rat that leaves
the town," said the Pied Piper.

A murmur ran through the crowd.

"A gold piece for each rat!" cried the mayor. "But that's impossible!
There must be several hundred or even several thousand rats in Hamelin!"

"There are a million of them," said the Pied Piper calmly. "And I will
not work for less than a million gold pieces."

"I need to think this over. I will call together my councillors. It is an
enormous sum that you are asking for!"

"I give you until tomorrow morning," replied the Piper with a smile.

The mayor summoned his councillors urgently.

"This man is our last hope. But paying him a gold piece for each rat seems a huge amount of money," he told them.

"We will have to raise the taxes. The people won't like that and will choose another mayor," said one of the councillors.

"Wait a minute, who's talking about paying him?" cried the mayor. "We can easily accept his suggestion, let him do his work, and then drive him out of the town without paying him anything."

All the councillors clapped and the mayor returned to the town hall square, satisfied with his mean plan. He found the Piper sitting by the fountain, polishing his flute.

"Stranger," said the mayor, "we are agreed. We will pay the price you ask if you succeed in getting rid of the rats. When can you begin?"

"This very night," said the Piper. "Order everyone to stay indoors."

The mayor went home, very proud of his plan. The townsfolk of Hamelin were lucky to have such a clever mayor! His wife and six sons were waiting for him at home, in tears. They had spent all day trying to drive the rats out of their house, but in vain.

"Don't worry. Tomorrow this nightmare will be over, there won't be a single rat left in the town," promised the mayor.

23

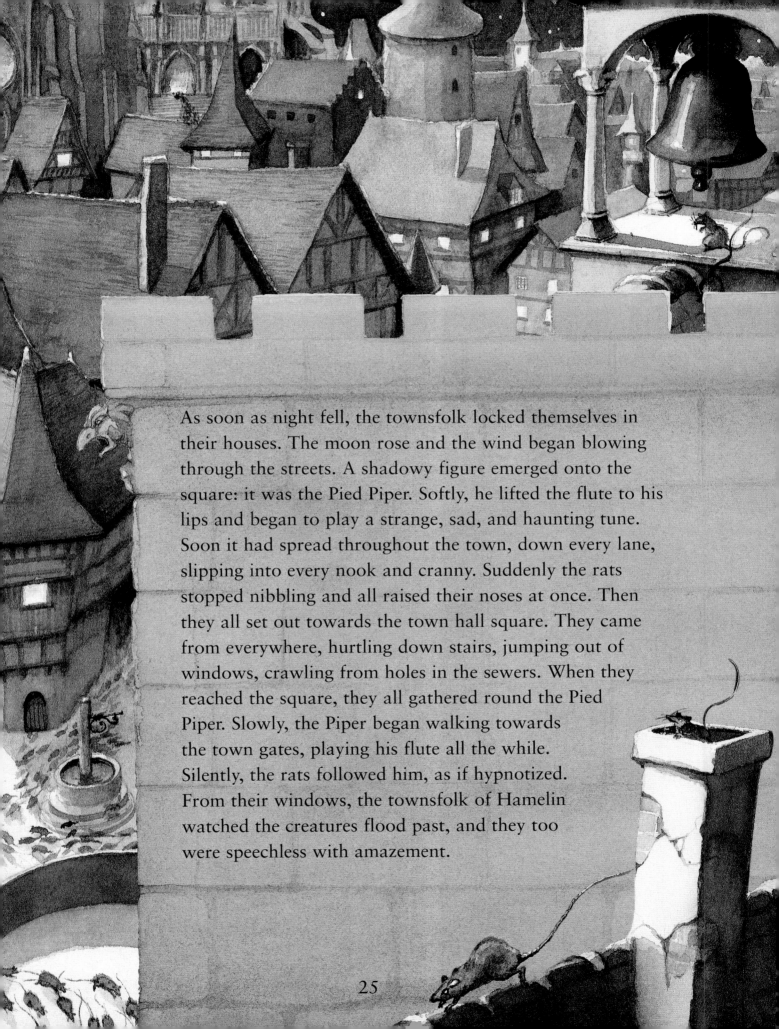

As soon as night fell, the townsfolk locked themselves in
their houses. The moon rose and the wind began blowing
through the streets. A shadowy figure emerged onto the
square: it was the Pied Piper. Softly, he lifted the flute to his
lips and began to play a strange, sad, and haunting tune.
Soon it had spread throughout the town, down every lane,
slipping into every nook and cranny. Suddenly the rats
stopped nibbling and all raised their noses at once. Then
they all set out towards the town hall square. They came
from everywhere, hurtling down stairs, jumping out of
windows, crawling from holes in the sewers. When they
reached the square, they all gathered round the Pied
Piper. Slowly, the Piper began walking towards
the town gates, playing his flute all the while.
Silently, the rats followed him, as if hypnotized.
From their windows, the townsfolk of Hamelin
watched the creatures flood past, and they too
were speechless with amazement.

The Piper walked to the river Weser, which ran outside the town. He stopped at the water's edge and looked at the mass of rats spread out before him, every one of them staring at him with beady eyes. Suddenly he shouted:

"Jump!"

Without a moment's hesitation, all the rats flung themselves into the freezing water and disappeared. When not a single rat was left on the bank, the Pied Piper stopped and returned to the town.

Next morning, the Pied Piper knocked on the mayor's door. After a long pause, the mayor answered. He was still in his dressing gown and nightcap.

"There is not a single rat left in the town," announced the Piper. "I have come to claim what is owed to me: a million gold pieces."

"And where have the rats gone? How can I tell that they have gone for good?" asked the mayor.

"I drowned them in the Weser. I kept my part of the bargain. Now you must pay me," the stranger insisted.

"What? I must pay for disappearing rats! I told you I would pay a gold piece for each rat, but I meant real dead ones. You were supposed to bring them to me!"

With that, the mayor slammed the door. The Pied Piper stared with his piercing eyes at the door that had been shut in his face. Inside he heard a small child talking in his sleep and an idea took shape in his mind.

"I will find a way of making them pay for my services," he muttered. And he turned on his heel and walked away.

A little later, the mayor, in a very good mood, went to the town hall and called all the townsfolk to the square. When everyone had arrived, he spoke:

"Dear fellow citizens, today there is not a single rat left in the town! To celebrate this success, I invite you all to a great feast tonight at the town hall." That evening, the people of Hamelin got ready to attend the mayor's feast. They put their children to bed and went off to the town hall. There they drank, ate, and danced all night. Meanwhile, the Pied Piper walked alone through the town.

27

The moon rose and a fresh little wind began blowing. The Piper lifted his flute and began to play a merry, lively tune that spread even to the darkest alleyways. Suddenly the house doors opened…

28

...and the children poured out to gather round the
Pied Piper. Then he began walking towards the town gates, playing all
the while. The children followed, smiling and humming. They did not
take their eyes off him, just as if they had been hypnotized. Soon,
the Piper came to the river Weser. He crossed the bridge
with all the children and began climbing the
mountain on the other side. Still the children
followed him and did not seem to feel
tired. The bigger ones carried the
smaller ones and they were all
laughing and dancing together.
Soon, every one of them had
disappeared into the night.

Early next morning, when the townsfolk of Hamelin returned home, they searched for their children. The mayor of Hamelin ran through all the rooms of his house, desperately calling for his six sons, but they had gone. Then he found a piece of paper nailed to his door, on which was written:

"Received in payment for the disappearance of one million rats: 253 children from the town of Hamelin."

It was signed: "The Pied Piper."

The mayor became wild with distress. The children of Hamelin were never seen again, but even today, on misty evenings, when the moon rises and a fresh little wind begins blowing, far off in the mountain, you can hear a strange tune played on a flute and the echo of children's laughter. From that day on, the mayor of Hamelin always kept his promises, down to the last detail.

THE END

History of Hansel and Gretel

The modern tale of "Hansel and Gretel" was first written down by German authors the Brothers Grimm in the early 19th century from a story they heard in the German town of Cassel. It was they who named the children Hansel and Gretel. In earlier versions of the tale, the boy and girl were called Little Brother and Little Sister. Stories of children meeting witches in forests have been around for centuries.

Earlier tales similar to the "Hansel and Gretel" story include one by the French author Charles Perrault called "Le Petit Poucet" (Little Thumb) in 1697 in which children are abandoned in the woods by their parents. In 1698, another French writer, Madame d'Aulnoy wrote "Finette Cendron" (Cunning Cinders) in which three princesses are abandoned by their parents in a forest and discover a giant's house. One of the princesses leaves trails to find her way back through the forest, but the birds eat the final trail she lays down. Later on in the story, the ogre is tricked into an oven and is killed. The princesses escape and live happily ever after.

Many German fairy tales feature forests, since much of the country was covered in thick woods in the early 19th century. The forest was a fearsome and unknown place in which the imagination could go wild and anything could happen.

Originally the gingerbread house was just a house of bread. Bread was a rich enough food for many even a hundred years ago. It is only in the past hundred years that the bread turned to gingerbread in the story, probably because the tale is set in Germany and the country is known for its gingerbread.

The moral of the story is that you can succeed even if the problems are huge. Hansel and Gretel won in the end even though they faced frightening problems, from the evil stepmother who abandoned them to the witch who trapped them.

There was a German opera for children based on the tale in 1893, and this was incredibly successful. The story became more popular afterward. The opera doesn't have the parents abandoning the children—the children just find themselves lost in the forest.

31

History of The Pied Piper of Hamelin

In 1300, there was a stained-glass window in the church of Hamelin, Germany, that showed a pied piper and children dressed in white. It is said that the window was created when the children left the town. There is a written record of this sad event from 1384, which backs up the story, though no one knows why the children left. There is a German book dating from around 1440—1450 that tells of the event. It says: "In the year of 1284, on the days of saints John and Paul on 26 June, 130 children born in Hamelin were led by a piper, dressed in all kinds of colors, and lost." So this fairy tale may be based on a true event, although the story may have changed when it was being passed down from person to person through the years, and the rats were definitely added as an extra to the story.

In 1816, the German authors the Brothers Grimm wrote a fairy tale collection that included "The Children of Hamelin." In their version, only two children returned—one was blind and so wasn't able to tell the townsfolk where the children were; the other couldn't speak so couldn't tell the townsfolk where the Piper had taken them. The Pied Piper led the children down a dark tunnel into Transylvania (a region of Romania).

The English poet Robert Browning wrote a poem, probably based on the Grimms' story, called "The Pied Piper of Hamelin" in 1849, and this became very popular.

The fairy tale is unusual because it doesn't have a happy ending—no one knows what happened to the children of Hamelin. It is a mystery that still remains unsolved.

Even today there is a street in Hamelin called Bungelose Gasse (Drumless Lane) in which no one has been allowed to play music or sing for centuries. Around the world, the story has been made into plays, musical theater productions, books, poems, songs, and movies.